Pippin No Lickin'

Pippin No Lickin'

Published in New York, New York, by Morgan James Publishing. Morgan James is a trademark of Morgan James, LLC. www.MorganJamesPublishing.com

The Morgan James Speakers Group can bring authors to your live event. For more information or to book an event visit The Morgan James Speakers Group at www.TheMorganJamesSpeakersGroup.com.

ISBN 9781683509561 paperback
ISBN 9781683509578 eBook
Library of Congress Control Number: 2018934769

Cover and Interior Design by:
Christopher Kirk
www.GFSstudio.com

In an effort to support local communities, raise awareness and funds, Morgan James Publishing donates a percentage of all book sales for the life of each book to Habitat for Humanity Peninsula and Greater Williamsburg.

Get involved today! Visit www.MorganJamesBuilds.com

Pippin No Lickin'

Layne Ihde

Illustrations by Linda Pierce

NEW YORK

LONDON • NASHVILLE • MELBOURNE • VANCOUVER

About the Author

Layne Ihde is an author and musician who lives in Nashville, Tennessee, with his wife and cat, a white tabby named Lizzie. He writes all different kinds of stories: children's books, songs, short stories and poems. His website is www.LayneIhde.com. He is also a member of a kids' rock band called The Happy Racers. You can find out more about them at www.thehappyracers.com.

About the Illustrator

Artist/Illustrator Linda Pierce of Rock Hill Farm Studio has been drawing for kids for some 30+ years, and has done work for nearly every publisher in the US and abroad. A BFA from the Rhode Island School of Design studying under such instructors as Chris Van Allsburg ("Polar Express, Jumanji"), and David Macaulay ("How Things Work"), has made for a well rounded career. She is also a professional Portrait Painter. www.rockhillfarmstudio.com.

For Erin, Lizzie and my family.

Cats know to bathe from the minute they're born.
If their mamas don't show them, they'd still somehow learn.

But Pippin was different, he didn't like preening,
he'd rather do anything else than self-cleaning.

"Your fur will get sticky!" his mama would say.
And papa said, "Things may get caught there and stay!"

And the kids in his class were all starting to feel
the smell from his coat would soon make the paint peel.

But he wouldn't listen, he went his own way
until some odd things started happening one day.

He was walking along just humming a tune,
felt something and turned, a red plastic kazoo

was stuck just behind his right shoulder of fuzz,
but hey, it was there if he wanted to buzz!

A little bit later his tail felt like a ton,
he looked back to see a huge chunk of grape gum!

"Oh well," Pippin thought, as he sniffed and then licked it,
it still had some flavor, he'd save it a bit.

Passing a puddle, he caught his reflection,
saw something yellow in the general direction
of the top of his ear, a dandelion perched
and it wouldn't budge for how hard he lurched.

"Hmm," said Pippin, "I don't think that I mind that,
it's pretty cool there, it's kind of a hat!"

The next day mid-morning he felt something prickle
and there on his back an orange butterfly tickled.

As its wings fluttered he felt pretty proud,
he had his own fan so he grinned and meowed.

By the day and the time of his grade school class pictures he'd quite the collection of fur-sticky fixtures.

The things he had added since leaving from home
were now a green grub, white wrapper, blue comb!

His teacher said, "Pippin, it's really an issue.
I think that the class has something to tell you."

Then Amanda the panda stood up with conviction and spoke with her best politeness and diction.

"Pippin, you know that we like you a lot,
but to say that we're fans of not bathing, we're not.
We can't last much longer, we need a real breather.
We don't really want dirty stuff on us, either."

Pippin said, "Look guys, I'm really not crazy.
I guess that it's just I'm a little bit lazy.

But I didn't get
it's not just about me.
It affects other people
I'm starting to see.

So I will clean off all these items and bugs."
Then they all gathered 'round and gave him "air hugs."

When Pippin got home he promptly exclaimed,
"Hey mama, hey papa I'm making a change.